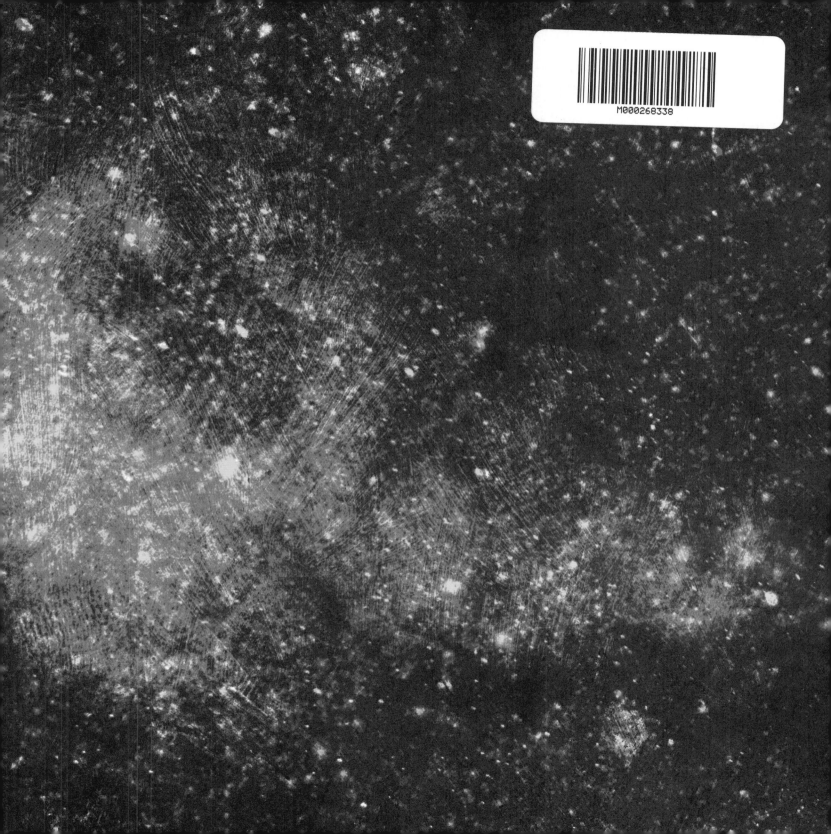

STAR TREK®

A VERY KLINGON
KHRISTMAS

Gallery Books
A Division of Simon & Schuster, Inc.
1230 Avenue of the Americas
New York, NY 10020

For information about special discounts for bulk purchases, please contact Simon & Schuster Special Sales at 1-866-506-1949 or business@simonandschuster.com.

Printed in China by Hung Hing.

10 9 8 7 6 5 4 3 2 1

Library of Congress Cataloging-in-Publication Data is available.

ISBN: 978-14767-4680-7

A Very Klingon Khristmas is produced by becker&mayer!, Bellevue, Washington.
www.beckermayer.com

Editor: Dana Youlin
Designer: Sam Dawson
Production coordinator: Tom Miller
Managing editor: Michael del Rosario
Illustrator: Patrick Faricy

Special thanks to Risa Kessler for developing this concept.

STAR TREK

A VERY KLINGON
KHRISTMAS

PAUL RUDITIS

ILLUSTRATED BY PATRICK FARICY

'Tis only on Khristmas
we Klingons feel mirth—
the day of the warrior,
Kahless's birth.
The most fearless of fighters
we'll never forget.
For his equal among us
has never been met.

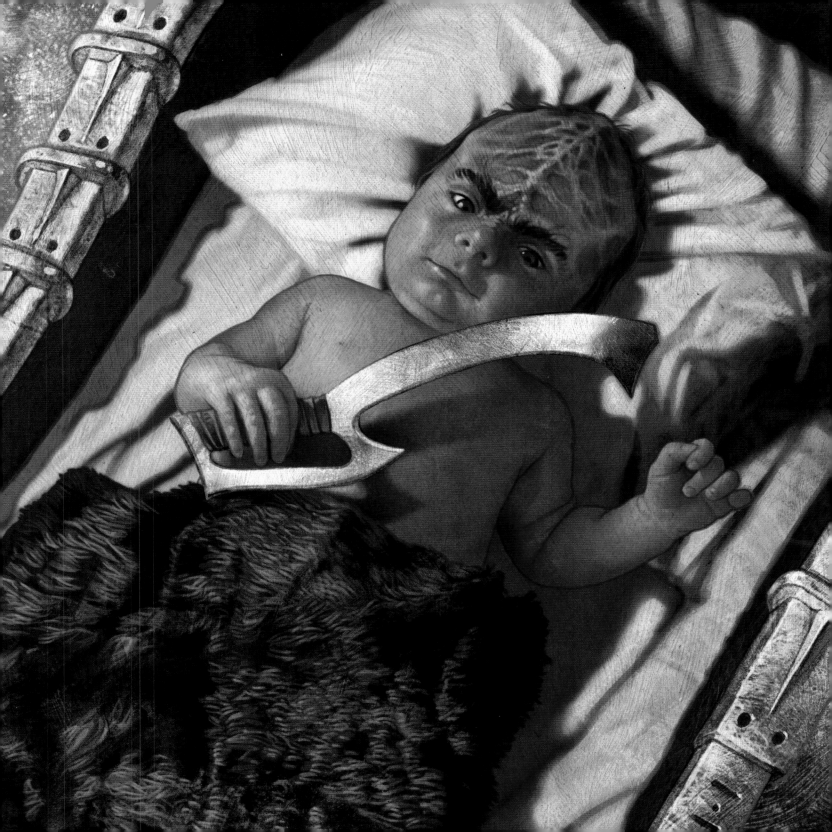

This story is known
by us all, near and far,
of the leader who swore
to return on a star.
But the one day that Klingons
all hold the most dear
has been stolen by humans,
just like our Shakespeare!

taH pagh taHbe'

They took our tradition,
our hero, our rites,
our bright decorations . . .
our Khristmas tree lights.
They've changed up our story—
they've got it all mangled
in much the same way that
our lights become tangled!

It is true we praise Kahless
in music and song,
shouting out battle carols
for all the night long.
These songs might not
start out sounding so fine,
but they always get better
with hot mulled blood wine.

ej HumtaH 'ej DechtaH 'Iw
'ej Doq SoDtaH ghoSpa' Sqral bIQtIq
'e' pa' jaj law' mo' jaj puS
jaj qeylIS molar mIgh HoHchu'qu

Then on Khristmas Eve night
we await Santa Qlas.
But our Kringle's equipped
with retractable claws.
He, too, makes a list
of who's naughty and nice.
But he doesn't waste time
with checking it twice.

He sees who is sleeping
and knows who's awake.
His scanners and sensors
aren't easy to shake.
Though Santa is fearsome,
he also brings joy.
He brings something special
for each girl and each boy.
There's dollies and yo-yos,
toy trains with conductors,
and maybe a *mek'leth*
or pair of disruptors.

He carries them all
in a warp-twenty sleigh,
led through the night
by eight tiny birds-of-prey
(and sometimes a ninth
that will help clear the way).

On, Ch'Tang! On, Ki'Tang!
On, M'Char! And Slivin!

Neither barring the doors
nor the chimney will do.
Santa's transporter beams
him right through.
But houses are ready,
they've all left him snacks;
some *gagh* and some *racht*
for his hunger attacks.

The kids sneak downstairs
for their one chance to see
Santa Qlas putting
all their gifts beneath the tree.
Laying finger on combadge
that sits on his chest,
he beams back to his sleigh
to bring toys to the rest.

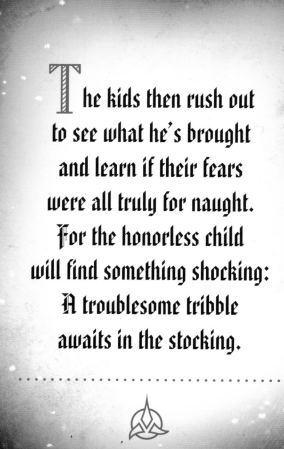

The kids then rush out
to see what he's brought
and learn if their fears
were all truly for naught.
For the honorless child
will find something shocking:
A troublesome tribble
awaits in the stocking.

But the brave Klingon tykes
will have nothing to dread
from the visions of evil
that dance in their heads.
When the children begin
to play with their new toys,
parents send them outside
to escape from the noise.

· ·

Just like Earth kids,
they have fun in the snow,
making snowgons and
weaponized snowballs to throw.
Before long they'll head home
escaping the cold.
Klingons hate winter;
so fast it gets old!

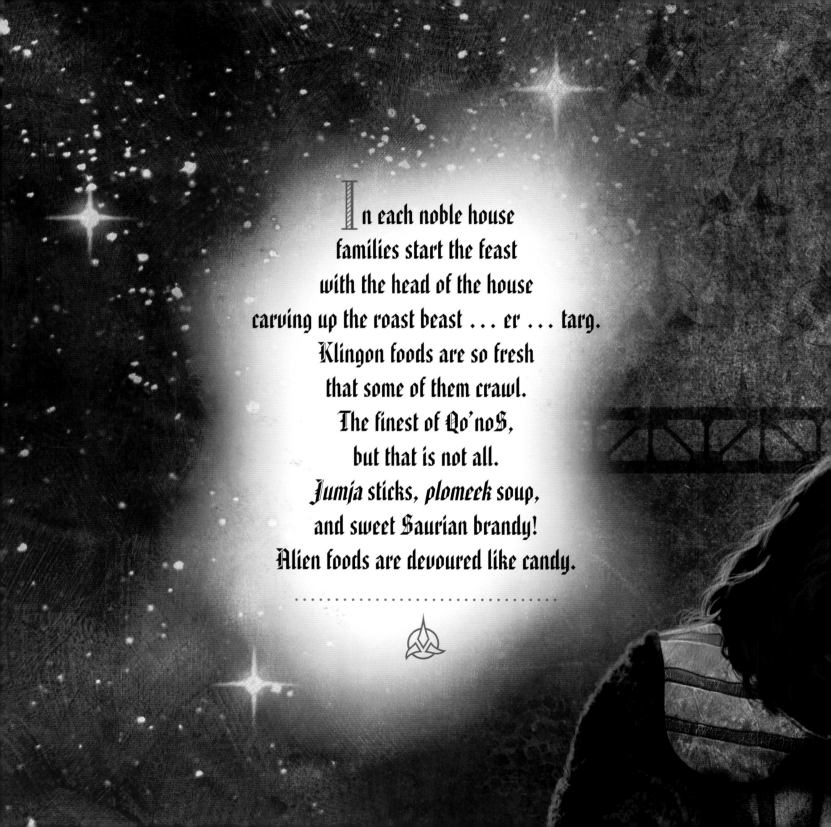

In each noble house
families start the feast
with the head of the house
carving up the roast beast ... er ... targ.
Klingon foods are so fresh
that some of them crawl.
The finest of Qo'noS,
but that is not all.
Jumja sticks, *plomeek* soup,
and sweet Saurian brandy!
Alien foods are devoured like candy.

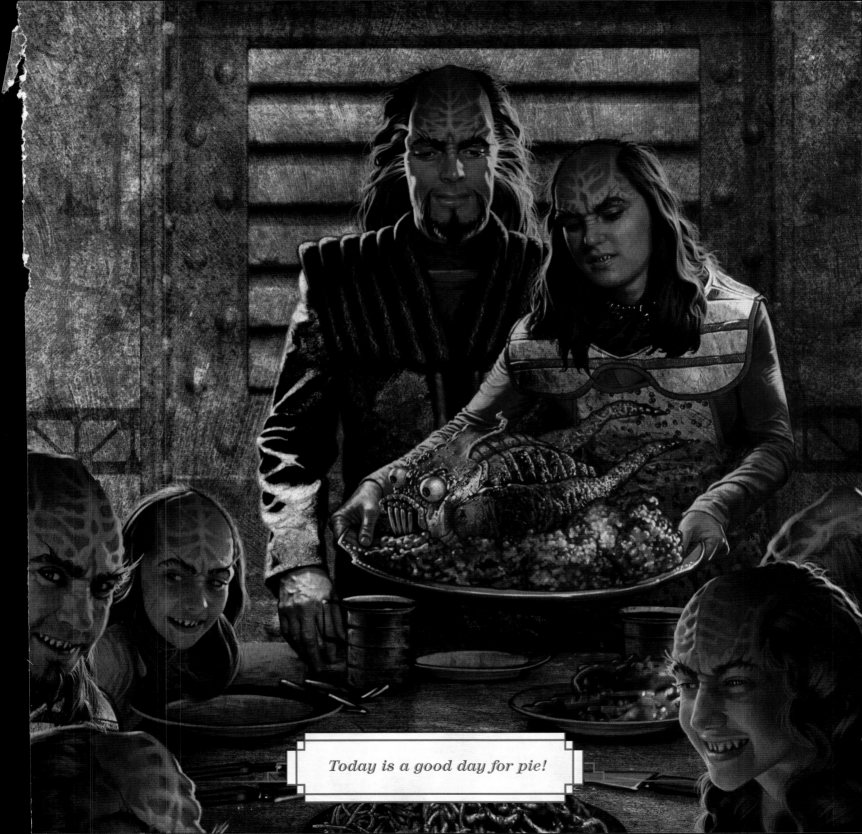

Today is a good day for pie!

See the couple canoodle
below mistletoe.
If he survives courting,
he'll become her new beau.
The leaves twinkle green,
and the berries shine redly.
Only Klingons could love
a plant that's so deadly.

Santa watches it all from the stars up above,
celebrating the day filled with honor and love.
With a shout of "Qapla'!" his sleigh quickly departs.
Coordinates set on his private star charts.
And he's heard to exclaim in the night still and calm,
"Happy Khristmas to all, and to all a *maj ram!*"